Horton Hatches the Egg

Dr. Seuss

HarperCollins *Children's Books*

CONDITIONS OF SALE

This book is sold subject to the condition that it shall not, by way of
trade or otherwise, be lent, re-sold, hired out or otherwise circulated
without the publisher's written consent in any form of binding or cover
other than that in which it is published and without a similar condition,
including this condition being imposed on the subsequent purchaser.

16 18 20 19 17

ISBN-10: 0-00-717519-1
ISBN-13: 978-0-00-717519-2

Horton Hatches the Egg
© 1940, 1968 by Dr. Seuss Enterprises, L.P.
All Rights Reserved
First published by Random House Inc.,
New York, USA
First published in the UK 1962
This edition published in the UK 2003 by
HarperCollins*Children's Books*,
a division of HarperCollins*Publishers* Ltd
77-85 Fulham Palace Road
London W6 8JB

Visit our website at:
www.harpercollins.co.uk

Printed and bound in Hong Kong

Sighed Mayzie, a lazy bird hatching an egg:
"I'm tired and I'm bored
And I've kinks in my leg
From sitting, just sitting here day after day.
It's *work!* How I hate it!
I'd *much* rather play!
I'd take a vacation, fly off for a rest
If I could find *someone* to stay on my nest!

If I could find someone, I'd fly away—free. . . ."

Then Horton, the Elephant, passed by her tree.

"Hello!" called the lazy bird, smiling her best,
"You've nothing to do and I *do* need a rest.
Would YOU like to sit on the egg in my nest?"

The elephant laughed.
"Why, of all silly things!
I haven't feathers and *I* haven't wings.
ME on your egg? Why, that doesn't make sense. . . .
Your egg is so small, ma'am, and I'm so immense!"

"Tut, tut," answered Mayzie. "I know you're not small
But I'm *sure* you can do it. No trouble at all.
Just sit on it softly. You're gentle and kind.
Come, be a good fellow. I know you won't mind."

"I can't," said the elephant.
"PL-E-E-ASE!" begged the bird.
"I won't be gone long, sir. I give you my word.
I'll hurry right back. Why, I'll never be missed. . . ."

"Very well," said the elephant, "since you insist. . . .

You want a vacation. Go fly off and take it.
I'll sit on your egg and I'll try not to break it.
I'll stay and be faithful. I mean what I say."

"Toodle-oo!" sang out Mayzie and fluttered away.

"H-m-m-m . . . the first thing to do," murmured Horton,
"Let's see. . . .
The first thing to do is to prop up this tree
And make it much stronger. That *has* to be done
Before I get on it. I must weigh a ton."

Then carefully,
Tenderly,
Gently he crept
Up the trunk to the nest where the little egg slept.

Then Horton the elephant smiled. "Now that's that. . . ."

And he sat
      and he sat
           and he sat
              and he sat. . . .

And he sat all that day
And he kept the egg warm. . . .
And he sat all that night
Through a *terrible* storm.
It poured and it lightninged!
It thundered! It rumbled!
"This isn't much fun,"
The poor elephant grumbled.
"I wish she'd come back
'Cause I'm cold and I'm wet.
I hope that that Mayzie bird doesn't forget."

But Mayzie, by this time, was far beyond reach,
Enjoying the sunshine way off in Palm Beach,
And having *such* fun, such a wonderful rest,

Decided she'd NEVER go back to her nest!

So Horton kept sitting there, day after day.
And soon it was Autumn. The leaves blew away.
And then came the Winter . . . the snow and the sleet!
And icicles hung
From his trunk and his feet.

But Horton kept sitting, and said with a sneeze,
"I'll *stay* on this egg and I *won't* let it freeze.
I meant what I said
And I said what I meant. . . .
An elephant's faithful
One hundred per cent!"

So poor Horton sat there
The whole winter through. . . .
And then came the springtime
With troubles anew!
His friends gathered round
And they shouted with glee.

"Look! Horton the Elephant's
Up in a tree!"
They taunted. They teased him.
They yelled, "How absurd!"
"Old Horton the Elephant
Thinks he's a bird!"

They laughed and they laughed. Then they all ran away.
And Horton was lonely. He wanted to play.
But he sat on the egg and continued to say:
"I meant what I said
And I said what I meant. . . .
An elephant's faithful
One hundred per cent!

"No matter WHAT happens,
This egg must be tended!"

But poor Horton's troubles
Were far, far from ended.
For, while Horton sat there
So faithful, so kind,
*Three hunters came sneaking
Up softly behind!*

He heard the men's footsteps!
He turned with a start!
Three rifles were aiming
Right straight at his heart!

Did he run?
He did not!
HORTON STAYED ON THAT NEST!
He held his head high
And he threw out his chest
And he looked at the hunters
As much as to say:
"Shoot if you must
But I *won't* run away!
I meant what I said
And I said what I meant. . . .
An elephant's faithful
One hundred per cent!"

But the men *didn't* shoot!
Much to Horton's surprise,
They dropped their three guns
And they stared with wide eyes!
"Look!" they all shouted,
"Can such a thing be?
An elephant sitting on top of a tree . . ."

"It's strange! It's amazing! It's wonderful! New!
Don't shoot him. We'll CATCH him. That's *just* what we'll do!
Let's take him alive. Why, he's terribly funny!
We'll sell him back home to a circus, for money!"

And the first thing he knew, they had built a big wagon
With ropes on the front for the pullers to drag on.
They dug up his tree and they put it inside,
With Horton so sad that he practically cried.
"We're off!" the men shouted. And off they all went
With Horton unhappy, one hundred per cent.

Up out of the jungle! Up into the sky!
Up over the mountains ten thousand feet high!
Then down, down the mountains
And down to the sea
Went the cart with the elephant,
Egg, nest and tree . . .

Then out of the wagon
And onto a ship!
Out over the ocean . . .
And oooh, what a trip!
Rolling and tossing and splashed with the spray!
And Horton said, day after day after day,
"I meant what I said
And I said what I meant . . .
But oh, am I seasick!
One hundred per cent!"

After bobbing around for two weeks like a cork,
They landed at last in the town of New York.
"All ashore!" the men shouted,
And down with a lurch
Went Horton the Elephant
Still on his perch,
Tied onto a board that could just scarcely hold him. .

BUMP!
Horton landed!
And then the men sold him!

Sold to a circus! Then week after week
They showed him to people at ten cents a peek.
They took him to Boston, to Kalamazoo,
Chicago, Weehawken and Washington, too;
To Dayton, Ohio; St. Paul, Minnesota;
To Wichita, Kansas; to Drake, North Dakota.
And everywhere thousands of folks flocked to see
And laugh at the elephant up in a tree.
Poor Horton grew sadder the farther he went,
But he said as he sat in the hot noisy tent:
"I meant what I said, and I said what I meant . . .
An elephant's faithful—one hundred per cent!"

Then . . . ONE DAY
The Circus Show happened to reach
A town way down south, not so far from Palm Beach.
And, dawdling along way up high in the sky,
Who (*of all people!*) should chance to fly by
But that old good-for-nothing bird, runaway Mayzie!
Still on vacation and still just as lazy.
And, spying the flags and the tents just below,
She sang out, "What fun! Why, I'll go to the show!"

And she swooped from the clouds
Through an open tent door . . .
"Good gracious!" gasped Mayzie,
"I've seen YOU *before!"*

Poor Horton looked up with his face white as chalk!
He started to speak, but before he could talk . . .

There rang out the noisiest ear-splitting squeaks
From the egg that he'd sat on for fifty-one weeks!
A thumping! A bumping! A wild alive scratching!
"My egg!" shouted Horton. "My EGG! WHY, IT'S HATCHING!"

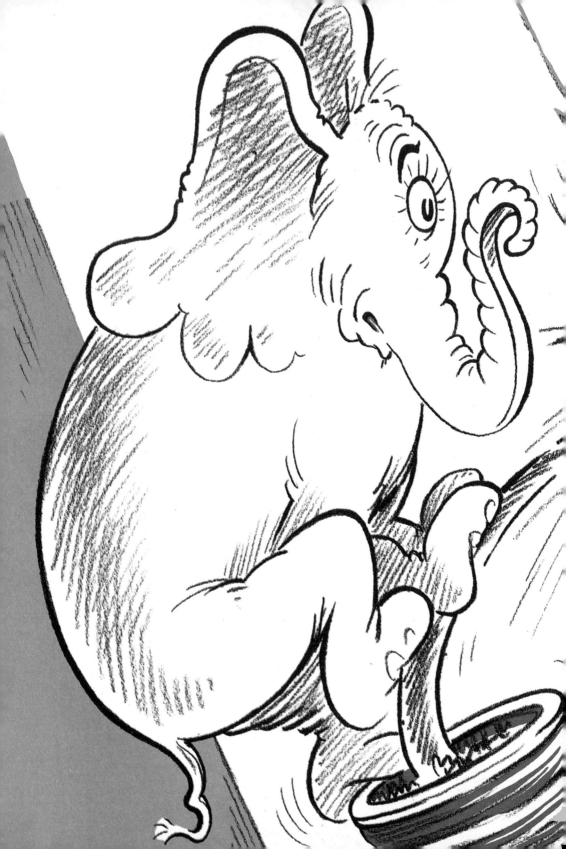

"But it's MINE!" screamed the bird, when she heard the egg crack.
(The work was all done. Now she wanted it back.)
"It's MY egg!" she sputtered. "You stole it from me!
Get off of my nest and get out of my tree!"

Poor Horton backed down
With a sad, heavy heart. . . .

But at that very instant, the egg burst apart!
And out of the pieces of red and white shell,
From the egg that he'd sat on so long and so well,
Horton the Elephant saw something whizz!
IT HAD EARS

AND A TAIL

AND A TRUNK JUST LIKE HIS!

And the people came shouting, *"What's all this about . . .?"*
They looked! And they stared with their eyes popping out!
Then they cheered and they *cheered* and they CHEERED more and more.
They'd never seen anything like it before!
"My goodness! *My gracious!*" they shouted. "MY WORD!
It's something brand new!
IT'S AN ELEPHANT-BIRD!!

And it should be, it *should* be, it SHOULD be like that!

Because Horton was faithful! He sat and he sat!

He meant what he said

And he said what he meant. . . ."

. . . And they sent him home
Happy,
One hundred per cent!

Read them **together**, read them **alone**, read them **aloud** and make **reading fun!**
With over **50 wacky stories** to choose from, now it's **easier** than **ever** to find the
right **Dr. Seuss** books for your child – just let the **back cover colour** guide you!

Here's a great selection to choose from:

Blue back books
for sharing with your child

Dr. Seuss's ABC
A Fly Went By
The Bears' Picnic
The Bike Lesson
The Eye Book
The Foot Book
Go, Dog, Go!
Hop on Pop
I'll Teach My Dog 100 Words
Inside Outside Upside Down
Mr. Brown Can Moo! Can You?
One Fish, Two Fish, Red Fish, Blue Fish
The Shape of Me and Other Stuff
There's a Wocket in my Pocket!

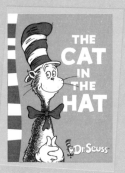

Green back books
for children just beginning to read on their own

A Fish Out of Water
And to Think That I Saw It on Mulberry Street
Are You My Mother?
The Bears' Holiday
Bears On Wheels
The Best Nest
The Cat in the Hat
The Cat in the Hat Comes Back
Come Over To My House
The Digging-est Dog
Fox in Socks
Gerald McBoing Boing
Green Eggs and Ham
Happy Birthday to YOU
Hunches in Bunches
I Can Read With My Eyes Shut!
I Wish That I Had Duck Feet
Marvin K. Mooney Will You Please Go Now!
Oh, Say Can You Say?
Oh, the Thinks You Can Think!
Ten Apples Up on Top
Wacky Wednesday

Yellow back books
for fluent readers to enjoy

The 500 Hats of Bartholomew Cubbins
Daisy-Head Mayzie
Did I Ever Tell You How Lucky You Are?
Dr. Seuss's Sleep Book
Horton Hatches the Egg
Horton Hears a Who!
How the Grinch Stole Christmas!
If I Ran the Circus
If I Ran the Zoo
I Had Trouble in Getting to Solla Sollew
The Lorax
McElligot's Pool
Oh, the Places You'll Go!
On Beyond Zebra
Scrambled Eggs Super!
The Sneetches and other stories
Thidwick the Big-Hearted Moose
Yertle the Turtle and other stories

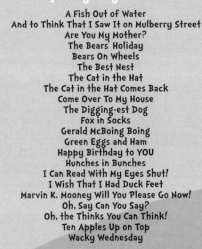